D1468684

WALKING ON GLASS

WALKING ON GLASS

Alma Fullerton

HarperTempest
An Imprint of HarperCollins*Publishers*

HarperTempest is an imprint of HarperCollins Publishers.

Walking on Glass
Copyright © 2007 by Alma Fullerton
Library of Congress Cataloging-in-Publication Data
Fullerton, Alma.
    Walking on glass / Alma Fullerton.—1st ed.
      p.   cm.
    Summary: A teenage boy recounts, in a free verse journal,
his attempts to come to terms with the realities of his
mother's near-death coma.
    ISBN-10: 0-06-077851-2 (trade bdg.)
    ISBN-13: 978-0-06-077851-4 (trade bdg.)
    ISBN-10: 0-06-077852-0 (lib. bdg.)
    ISBN-13: 978-0-06-077852-1 (lib. bdg.)
    [1. Emotional problems—Fiction. 2. Mothers and sons—
Fiction. 3. Conduct of life—Fiction. 4. Suicide—Fiction.
5. Diaries—Fiction. 6. Novels in verse.] I. Title.
PZ7.5.F85 Wal 2007   2006020037
[Fic]—dc22   CIP
                                                    AC

Typography by Amy Ryan
2 3 4 5 6 7 8 9 10

First Edition

For Jessica,

Chantale,

and Claude

for always being there

when I need them. Love you.

With special thanks to
Kim Marcus, Jennifer Jessup,
Mark McVeigh, Melanie Donovan,
Susan Ambert, and Leona Trainer
for helping me make this book happen.

WALKING ON GLASS

A PERSONAL JOURNAL

Date of journal—
between the start and finish

JUST TO LET
YOU KNOW

I begin this
under protest.

The further you read,
the more you invade my mind.

Take something from me
I don't want to give.

My thoughts.

You will enter a place
I don't want to be.

My conscience.

JOURNALS

Writing a journal
for some shrink
won't make me
feel better.
It won't change
what happened.
It'll just make me think,
and I don't want to think.
Mom thought too much.
Look where it got her.

THIS IS STUPID

Shit happens.
We have to
deal with it.
We can't
change it.
Why pick it apart
like a detective
dissects a suicide note.

BESIDES

Only girls
and wusses
write journals.
If Jack finds out
I'm writing one,
he'll hassle me so much
I'll have to beat the crap out of him
just to prove
I'm no wuss.

JACK

I know Mom hates him.
He hangs around
with the King's Crypt
and shows up
at our house
wasted.

But I don't care.

Jack has always been
my best friend.

He knows how
to have a good time.

ME AND JACK

Jack pulls up in a kick-ass
Mustang convertible.
He whoops as he gets out
and grins. "Not bad, hey?"

"Damn right," I say,
wishing I had the cash
to buy a car
like that.

"Come on," he says.

I jump in and we head downtown.
We pass some girls we've seen
at some parties,
so he turns around
and pulls up beside them.
"Want a ride?" he asks.

They jump in.

We speed through the streets,
blasting the music
and flipping off people who glare.

And for a while
I forget all about Mom.

MY SHRINK

I slouch in a chair
across from Dr. Mac.
He takes my journal
and flips through it
without reading,
like he promised.

"I'm glad you're writing."
He hands it back.
"How's your mother?"

I spin my chair, lean back,
and put my feet up on his desk.
"Same."

He nods, waiting for me to say more.
I don't, making him ask,
"How are you?"

I shrug. "Same."

THE WAY SHE WAS

I took the photograph
from the mirror in my mother's room.
Her at the age of eight,
perched high in a tree,
arms stretched out like
an untamed eagle,
prepared to take on
the world.

I keep the picture
in my pocket
so I'll always
remember
the way she was
before she was caged
by a baby
she never wanted.

THIS IS HOW IT IS

Dad says,
"Come and see Mom."
So I do.

Mom,
tucked tight in the bed,
empty minded.
No longer herself,
or anyone else.

Wires force life into a body
left hanging
like a marionette
with no one to pull
the strings.

Dad leans close to her
and whispers,
"You'll come home soon, dear.
Everything will be better."

I know he really
wants that
to be true,
but the thought of her
coming back
into our lives
makes my insides
flip.

PLEASE
UNDERSTAND

Mom's mood swings
always coincided
with whatever
Dad and I did.
Up and down.
Up and down.
Pulling our strings,
like big yo-yos.
And even now,
when she can't move
or talk,
she's still pulling
those strings.

HONESTLY

I don't want her to die.
I just want
it all to
stop.
Does that make me
so terrible?

ROSES

Mom loved
her roses.

They grew into
prizewinners,
nurtured by her long hours
and tender hands.
They brought her
a sense of fulfillment.

I just let her
down.

ALL GOOD
THINGS GONE

I wait outside
on the step for Jack.
Vines tangle
around Mom's roses
like bad times.

I yank at the weeds
and chuck them far
from the garden,
yelling, "Get Out!"

The nosy neighbor,
Mrs. Wingert,
peeks around her curtains.
She glares at me,
like she thinks
I've gone over the edge.

Maybe
I have.

I throw a handful of dirt
in her direction and scream,
"Mind your own damn business."

She drops her curtain closed,
but I can still feel her eyes
on the back of my head.

By the time Jack arrives,
weeds are scattered over the yard,
my hands are caked with mud,
and I have a headache
from clenching my teeth together
so tight.

IF THE SHOE FITS

Jack pulls into a
parking space near the lake.
He taps my chest and points to
a scrawny kid sprawled
across a bench reading.

"Want to have some fun?" he
whispers.

"Oh yeah," I go.

He struts over to the kid
and kicks his foot.
"Nice shoes.
Your mom buy them for you?"

The kid jumps to his feet
and glances around,
but the rest of the park
is deserted.

"I asked, did your
mom pay for them?"
Jack barks.

"I—I guess so."
The kid clutches his book
to his chest.

Jack shoves him down.
"I want them shoes."

"I d-don't have another pair."

"You hear that?" Jack says.
"He d-don't have another pair."
My laughter mixes with Jack's,
and he plows the kid in the face.

The kid covers his nose
as his blood gushes
through his fingers.

Jack turns to leave,
but that kid is staring at me
over his bloody fingers,
and I stand frozen.

I wish that kid would
stop.
But he doesn't.
He stares
like he knows
what my mother did.
He stares
like he knows
why she did it.

He stares,
like he's expecting me to be nice.

He just keeps staring.
I shift my feet
and look away.
But I can feel him
staring
with eyes the color of
Mom's.
Staring.

"Stop gawking,
you freak!" I say.

But he doesn't.

"Stop looking at me!"
I shove him hard against the bench.

The kid's head snaps back,
like someone pulled an elastic
attached to it.

Jack turns around.
He pounds the kid
across the chin.
The kid falls onto the grass,
bawling
and gripping the sides of his face.

Things slow down in my head.
A movie,
paused,
scene by scene,
as Jack stands over him,
kicking at his ribs,
without giving in.
All because I didn't like the kid
staring.

The look in Jack's eyes
scares me
because I know
the kid has had enough,
and no matter what I do,
Jack won't stop.

"Loser!" Jack rips off the kid's shoes.
He leaves him lying on the ground
bleeding.
He trots to his car,
carrying the shoes
over his head like a trophy.

I see the kid stagger to his
sock feet.
He wipes the blood
from under his nose.

That kid has to go home
and tell his mother
two guys beat him up
and stole his shoes.
And I want to puke.

IN THE CAR

Jack says, "What a riot."

I stare out the window,
not answering.

"You want the shoes?" he asks.

"No."

"You should take them.
Your shoes suck.
They keep falling off," he says.

"Mom bought me these shoes."
I look straight at him,
daring him to say something.

But he doesn't.
He just shrugs
and throws the shoes
on the backseat.

AT HOME

I curl up on my bed,
clutching my pillow.
Trickles of sweat
drip down the sides of my face.
I shiver.

My chest is locked
like an iron cage.
I gasp for air,
but the cage just
tightens.

Every time
I close my eyes,
I see blood
gushing from that kid's nose,
spilling onto his shoes,

and me laughing,
like some kind of an animal.

I grip the pillow tighter.
The cage grips me
hard enough to make
my heart pop.

I sob,
wishing my mother
was home
to open
the iron bars.
But she chose
not to be.

ANOTHER KID'S SHOES

That kid's shoes
are still in the back of Jack's car
untouched.

DOWNTOWN

There's a mural
painted on the side of
Mulier's Grocery.
An eagle.
Flying free.

Jack and I shake cans of paint
and spray lines through the eagle.
I step back, and it looks like a cage.

At home,
I stare at the ceiling,
thinking about Mom's photo.
The word *caged*
echoes through
my mind.

I race downtown
with soap and paint thinner.
Instead of freeing the eagle,
I smudge it into
nothing.

VISITING MOM

The beeping
from her machines
shrieks.

A reminder
her soul is tethered to the ground,
a captive falcon,
circling in confusion,
longing for someone
to set it
free.

I remember the Mulier's eagle
smudging away,
and I think maybe sometimes
nonexistence
is better than being
caged.

JUST DO IT

I stand watching her.
I want to smack her
for putting us through this.
I want to scream,
"Why didn't you want to live?
You're supposed to want to stay here
with us!"

If she's going to die,
she should get it over with
and just
do
it.

MAYBE

Dad's right.
Maybe
Mom will fight.
Maybe
she will come back.
Maybe
things will change.
Maybe . . .

A PARTY

Right now,
I want to party
as much as I want to
shove glass under my fingernails.

Jack says, "I'll pick you up."

So I go.

THE NEW GIRL

At the party
there's a
new girl.
Alissa.

Alissa
smiles at me.

I smile
back.

AM I?

Jack yells
at his mother.

Her tears dry
on the cold linoleum.
Like the blood
I found on the floor
of my house.

Later, I say,
"You should be nicer
to your mother."

Jack says,
"You're turning into a wuss
like your father."

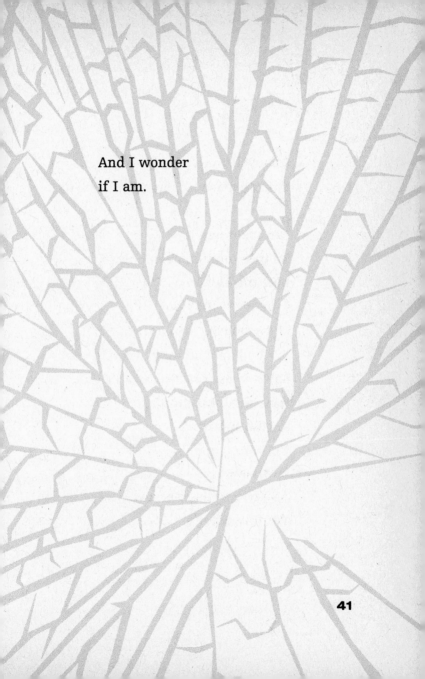

And I wonder
if I am.

JUST BECAUSE

I can't believe it.
Just because I blow up at some kid,
I have to see some
school counselor,
who is going to overanalyze
everything
I do.

It's bad enough that I have to see
Dr. Mac once a week,
because of my *stupid* mother.

I'm refusing to go.

ANXIETY ATTACKS

I have to dissolve
one tiny tablet
under my tongue
every night.
But unlike the pill,
the pain won't
melt away.

ALISSA'S SONG

Alissa sings in the choir.
A soloist,
with a voice
beautiful enough
to make anyone's problems
disappear.

Almost.

By the way,
I didn't mean it.
Mom's not
stupid.

WHAT'S WRONG
WITH ME?

I stand over Mom,
shaking inside,
and wonder why she did it.

Why she didn't think
about anyone
but herself.

Why she didn't think
about us.

Why she didn't think
about me.

AFTER SCHOOL

Jack and some of the Crypt
push around
some kids from the choir.
Alissa is there.

"Knock it off, Jack," I say.

"You gonna stop us?" he asks.

I don't answer.

"Loosen up."
Jack shoves my shoulder
and walks away.

JACK AND ME

I sit on my bed,
staring at the walls.
When we were eight,
Jack and I rode our bikes to the lake.
I remember having to pedal
against the wind
and was tired by the time we got
there.
When we were swimming,
a big wave washed over me
and was pulling me out
deeper into the lake.
Jack grabbed my arm.
He dragged me out of the water.
After that, we promised we'd be
best friends forever.

NURSES

Nurses lurk
around Mom's bed
like vultures.

But Dad guards her—
a lion
ready to pounce on
the vultures as they swoop
to take away his mate.

He doesn't seem to know
what the vultures
already know.

She's gone.

WALKING ON
BROKEN GLASS

If Mom came home,
things wouldn't change.
Her mood would always flip
from bad to worse
in a matter of seconds,
and for the rest of our lives
Dad and I would
be walking on
shards of glass
from a broken
chandelier.

ALISSA

After French class,
Alissa says, *"Bonjour.
Comment ça va?"*

I say, "Lahblah."

But she doesn't
seem to mind.

HOMEWORK

Dad says, "Do your homework.
It's important to get good grades
so you can go to college."

I won't go to college.

Mom's machines suck the
money out of our lives.

Leaving nothing.

MONEY

Jack has so much
money
now
he just buys things
without looking
at how much they cost.

THE CONVERSATION

When I was fourteen,
I was suspended from school
because I was caught with drugs.
Mom freaked.
She yelled, "Drugs will take you on
the road to nowhere.
They'll control your life
and you'll end up a nobody
behind caged walls.
Don't let anything trap
you like that."

I wonder if she knew then
that she'd be the one
to trap me.

TALKING

Dr. Mac asks,
"How is school?"

"Great."

"Do you have friends there?"

"There's the girl I like, Alissa,
and there's Jack."

"Jack's your best friend?"

"I guess," I say.

"You guess?"

"He's changing."

"How's that?" he asks.

I go on to tell him about
the look in Jack's eyes
when he beat that kid up.
And how he took his shoes.

"Why do you suppose
Jack would steal the shoes
for you?" Dr. Mac asks.

"Huh?"
I look at him,
confused.

IF I COULD GO BACK

My teacher asks everyone,
"If you could change
anything in history,
what would it be?"

Kids say things like,
I'd prevent wars
or Bin Laden and Hitler
wouldn't have been born.
Other kids nod their heads to agree.

When the teacher asks me,
I say,
"Four months ago,
I would have come home
five minutes earlier."

Everyone looks away from me
like my face is on
sideways.

THE HOUSE

It's too quiet
at home,
and it smells different.
There's no longer
the scent of the fresh flowers
Mom always kept
in the living room.
Instead I smell
dust, rot, and,
even after cleaning the floor,
blood.
Why can I still smell
the blood?

THE DATE

Jack calls.
"Come on a run with the gang.
We'll have a blast."

"I can't. I have a date
with Alissa."

"Pussy whipped,"
Jack jokes.

 I don't answer.

"Later then." He hangs up.

I borrow Dad's car
to pick up Alissa.

After the show she asks,
"How's your mother?"

"Same, I guess."

Without saying anything,
she takes my hand
and I notice I can
breathe.

AFTER MY DATE

Everything seems normal.
Like nothing has happened.
Like Mom never did it.
Like it's all a dream.
I look in Mom's room
and expect to find her there.
But she's not.

I pull her picture
out of my pocket
and rip it in half,
dropping it in the garbage
as I leave her room.

I'M SORRY

Clear tape
works miracles
on the back
of old photographs.

MOTHERS

Jack can't see
mothers are fragile
like a robin's egg
easily broken
by a child's hand.

Every day
I make sure
I'm extra nice
to Jack's mother.
So she knows
someone cares.

THINKING BACK

As I sit on the couch
staring at a cushion,
in silence,
I keep seeing Mom
curled up and gripping
this cushion on this couch,
alone,
crying
in the dark.

Instead of going to her,
I walked by.
Saying nothing,
like she was
invisible.

I hug the cushion

and smell it,
hoping to get a hint
of her perfume,
but it's gone.

All I can smell
is the
dust
left behind.

I go to my room,
take a pill,
and turn up the music
loud
so I can forget what
I remember.

NORMAL DAYS

Alissa and I
go to the
arcade.

We meet some
of her friends there
and play pool in teams.

They treat me like
they can't see the darkness
in the back of my mind
and I have
fun.

SPIRIT SCENTS

The wind blows
Mom's rose petals,
scattering them
across her garden—
unwanted children
tossed aside.

I gather the petals,
put them into a bowl,
and place it beside
Mom's bed.

They're dead,
but their scent fills the room
like a memory.

MY ARM

The force
of the chandelier
crashing down
broke my arm.

Even though
the glass has all been
swept away
and my arm is healed,
it still hurts
when it
rains.

HARD CORE

"This sucks.
I'm tired of being
some kind of wannabe."
Jack throws his beer bottle
under the graffiti
on the brick wall.
"I'm tired of it.
I'm going
hard core."

SLEEPLESS

My father
cries out to Mom
in his sleep.

I slide from the warmth
of my bed
to sleep on the bumpy couch
in the living room,
where I'll no longer
hear his calls.

ALISSA MEETS MOM

Alissa asks,
"Can I go with you
to meet your Mom?"

"I don't think she knows
we're there," I say.

"That's okay," she says.

"Whatever."

In Mom's hospital room,
Alissa sits beside her.

She takes Mom's hand gently,
like a veterinarian holds the
broken wing of a bird.

"Hello, I'm Alissa.
Pleased to finally meet you."

Her voice
overpowers the
squawks of the machines
until I can hear
nothing else.

STOLEN SOULS

What's left of the
old chandelier
is heaped next to the window.
And once in a while
the sun shines in
and rainbows dance
against the walls.

It's as if the crystals
stole Mom's spirit.

I hang the crystals
by the window
in Mom's room.

I hope they
give her
spirit
back.

THAT KID

I see the kid.
He's outside a white house
with a nice yard
and a dog.

He throws a football
with his father.
His mother comes outside smiling.
Carrying lunch.

Watching them,
I get the same feeling
I had when I was small
and Mom would chase me
in the backyard,
then pick me up,
wrapping me tight
in sheets straight off the line.

I wish *I had*
that kid's shoes.

WRINKLES

Dad looks
older than he is.
Wrinkles line
his tired eyes
and his hair
is turning
gray.

He doesn't smile
like he used to.
He won't look at me.

IDENTITY

In the smoke-filled room at Vic's,
Crypt members
and wannabes
gather,
drinking beer
and toking up.

Everyone is just one
big blob of blue
with no single
identity.

I can no longer
tell who is who.

SEVENTEEN

Jack turns
seventeen today.
He steals beer from his dad
and we go in the alley
behind the mall
to celebrate.

He drinks so much,
he stumbles.
People walk by,
laughing.

"Jack, let's go."
I grab his shoulders
and steer him out of the alley.

He sees this girl
and pushes me away.
"Waaaiit."

He grabs the girl's arm
and pulls her close to him.
He says he can bang her
so hard,
her eyeballs will roll
to the back of her head.

She tries to get away,
but he grabs her again.

I say,
"Leave her alone, Jack."
He doesn't.

Red marks spread
around his fingers as
they dig into her bare arm.

I yell,
"Let her go, Jack!"

He pulls her close
and licks the tears
off her face.

I hit him.
We're no longer
friends.

RELIEF

Today
the doctors tell Dad
there's still no hope.
Mom's not getting better.
They ask if he would
consent
to have the machines
shut down
and donate
Mom's organs.

Dad gets mad.
He refuses to believe
she's gone.

But I'm feeling
more relieved
than mad.

GOD, FORGIVE ME

The thought of my own mother
dying
shouldn't leave the taste of
freedom
in my mouth.

IS SHE THERE?

I sit with Mom
and squeeze her hand
gently.
Hoping she'll
squeeze back
like she used to when
I was small and
scared.

But no matter how often
I squeeze her hand,
it stays limp.

IN SCIENCE

Alissa sets all of the butterflies
free.

Colors fill the air
and float through
the school yard.

Mr. Crouch sends her
to the office for pulling a
stupid prank.

I don't think it was stupid.
I think it was
brave.

JACK'S MOTHER

I see Jack's mother
in the grocery store.
She asks, "How's your mom?"

"Same," I say.
I grab some TV dinners.

She picks through the frozen
vegetables
and says, "You should drop by for
supper.
We miss having you around."

I say, "I'm pretty busy."

"I understand." She looks past me,
far away.

MOM'S ROOM

Nurses flock
to Mom's room
like she's having a sale
on white sneakers.

In between their visits
I'm alone with her
and her machines.

I reach for the machine
to do what I need to do.

My hands shake,
and sweat drips
down the back of my legs,
stinging the open blisters
on my heels.

I jerk my hand away,
without even touching
the switch.

I race out of there,
gasping for air,
and throw up on
the shoes I still can't
fill.

QUESTIONS

"Do you ever feel like
someone's puppet?" I ask Dr. Mac.

He raises his eyebrows.
"Do you?"

I roll my eyes. "I asked you first."

"I think at times
we can all get our
strings pulled."

AVOIDING ALISSA

Alissa has the key
to the cage,
but I can't let
her open it
yet.

When the phone
rings and I see
Alissa's number
on the display,
I don't pick it up.

BREAKING AWAY

I trip over
Mom's shoes
at the bottom of the stairs.

I pick them up
and whip them through
the dining room window.

It shatters
over Mom's
precious rosebushes.

The cage
in my chest
loosens.

HIDDEN FROM VIEW

A board covers
the broken window
and I can no longer
see Mom's torn
roses.

DAD

Dad putters around the house
avoiding me.
I want to get right up
in his face
and scream for him
to be the man he should be
so I won't have to,
but I
can't.

ALISSA ASKS

"Why didn't you call?"

"I was busy."

"Is everything okay?"

"I think we shouldn't see each other
for a while."

"Why?"

I stare at my feet.
Her eyes are my looking glass,
able to flip the truth
and make me want to believe
everything is okay,
but it's not.

CONVERSATIONS
WITH DAD

"I know you think
I'm wrong,"
Dad says.

He looks at me
over the piles of
takeout containers
on the coffee table.

"I can't let go yet."

I scarf down my
chow-mein noodles
to avoid looking
directly at him.

"It's not my fault . . . ,"
he says.

I glance up.
His eyes water.
I focus my attention
on my noodles.

"And I didn't know she was that
unhappy," he says.

I push my plate
across the table.
It tips.

I get up
and walk away,
leaving my dad's heart
and the noodles
spilled all over the floor.

IN THE HALLWAY

At school
I see Alissa
talking to her friends.

I watch her
push her hair away
from her eyes.
Those beautiful
blue eyes, so full
of life.

Why can't I look
into them
and let her make
me feel
good again?

FORGIVENESS

Jack beats
on my front door.
"Come on!
I know you're home.
Let me in.
I forgive
you."

I don't get up.
He's not the one
who I need
to forgive
me.

ON THE WAY
TO SCHOOL

Jack catches up to me.

"What's with you
lately?" he asks.

"Nothing."

"Why you avoiding me then?"

I don't answer.
He knows why.

MIRRORS

Today
Dad smashes
the mirror
in the front hall.

I guess neither one
of us can stand to
look into it.

I SHOULD HAVE

As I left the house
that June morning,

Mom said,
"I love you."

I just closed the door
and left her
alone.

I should have told her
I loved her.
Maybe then
she wouldn't be
in the hospital
today.

WAITING FOR DEATH

I bring Mom
roses.

I watch her carefully,
looking for any clue
she knows I'm with her.

She lies there
lifeless.
I try to swallow the lump
building in my throat,
but it just expands.

The aroma from the roses
filters through the air.
They smell like she used to
when I was small.
Sweet and fresh.

Their scent
will fade
now that they're
no longer attached
to the roots
which gave them life.

I stare outside
and wonder
if I'll ever have the courage
to cut Mom off
from her roots.

THE PENALTY

In class today
we had a debate about
whether kids who kill
should be tried as adults.

Some of the class say
kids shouldn't be tried as adults
because we don't always know
right from wrong.

I think they're full of crap.
We do know right from wrong.

OPINION

I don't doubt for a second
that most people think
what I want to do
is wrong.
But I don't want to
murder
my mother.
I want to set her
free.

MURDER

The unlawful killing of a human
being
with malice
aforethought.

I'm thinking about it.
Does that make it
murder?

THINKING

Dr. Mac asks,
"What are you thinking?"

"Do you think that if
someone made your life
miserable,
unhooking that person's
life support
would be the same as murder,
even if you know
they will never get better?"

He leans forward
and looks into my eyes.
"It's not what I think
that's important.
It's what you think."

I WISH I MAY

Sometimes I wish
I hadn't held Mom up.
Then it would have
all been over
that rainy June day.

CLOSING DOORS

Jack comes by.
He says, "I need a place to stay.
Mom kicked me out
when I hit her."

But I just say,
"No."
And close the door.

FIRST SIGNS OF LIFE

Dad says,
"Jack isn't
coming by anymore."

I nod.

He smiles and pats me on the back,
and my cage bars
weaken.

MAYBE HE KNOWS

Dad sits beside
Mom's bed.
He strokes her hair
and whispers to her.
He closes his eyes.
Clenching his jaw,
he lets out a sigh.
When he opens his eyes,
a tear drips from each corner.
He shakes his head
and walks out of the room.

I wait for him to come back.
He doesn't.

DAD'S FEELINGS

I wonder
if Dad is torn up inside
for the same reason
I'm torn.

FLASHBACKS

Today
there I am
playing football
and suddenly it starts
to rain and I'm back
in time holding
my mother up
by her legs.

And I pray
I can hold her
long enough
to tell her
what she needs
to hear.

But before I
can get the words out,
I get tackled.

DEPRESSION

Today
Dr. Mac explains how
sick Mom was.
How she needed medicine
to make her feel better,
but she refused to take it.

He explains how,
if she did,
she'd still be here.

Today Dr. Mac
explains how
sick Mom was
and how nothing she did
was my
fault.

GANGS

I can't concentrate
on homework.
I watch the news
and hear about
a drive-by downtown.
A woman was killed
by a stray bullet.

They caught the shooter.
He's seventeen and
will be tried as
an adult.

COULD HAVE BEEN

My heart races,
thinking it could have been
me who killed that woman.

And I thank God
it wasn't.

It was Jack.

SURELY
IT'S DIFFERENT

Mom doesn't have
a future.
Mom doesn't have
a life.
Mom has been dead
for six months.
You can't call
it murder.

MOM'S ROSES

This morning
Mom's garden
froze over.

No one will cover
the fading roses.

Petals dropping
onto the frosty ground
like tears of

death.

MY DREAM

I dream about Jack
beating up that kid.
Blood dripping down his face
all over his shoes.
I watch confused,
knowing that didn't happen.
There wasn't blood
on those shoes.
Then it's my mother's face
and the blood drips
down onto my shoes.

I wake up screaming.
Because
I know
that happened.

WHAT HAPPENED

That day,
I came home and found
a new pair of shoes
by the door.
When I went into the dining room
to tell Mom they were
too big,
Mom stepped off of the table.
A noose slung around her neck.

I caught her
and held her up.

Mom struggled.
She kicked me away.

But I wouldn't
let go.

I wanted to tell her
I loved her.
I wanted to tell her
I needed her.
I wanted to tell her
to stay with us.

But the wires holding
the chandelier snapped,
and it crashed on top of her head,
and my arm broke
and I dropped her.

Her blood splattered
all over my new shoes.

REMEMBERING MOM

I remember
her soft voice
floating through the air
like the smell of fresh roses,
as she sings me a lullaby
to take away
the monsters in the night.

I remember
her dimpled smile,
her blue eyes,
her gentle touch.

I remember
my mother,
the way she was.

COVERING
MOM'S ROSES

Frost paints
the dining room window.
Outside
Mom's rosebushes
shiver as the wind
beats on their
bare branches.

I search through the
dark basement
to gather ragged
potato sacks.

I wrap them
around my mother's
precious plants.

Thorns pierce my hand
and blood drips down
the stem of the frozen bush
like the tears
on my face.

THIS IS NOT A LIFE

It's early,
but I go visit Mom
anyhow.
She lies on the bed.
Her hair plastered
to the sides of her head.
Machines drip liquid
into her veins,
feeding her.

The roses in her vase
are rotting and
she's
rotting
with
them.

THIS HAS
TO BE RIGHT

If the doctors say
she's not going to come back,
then shutting off the machines
wouldn't be killing her—
it'll just finish
what she has already
done.

MOM'S BIRTHDAY

The doctors take
Dad into another room,
leaving me alone
with the shell
of my mother.

I brush the hair from her face
and rest my hand
on her forehead.

I sit,
listening to the machines
as their parts move,
and I'm no longer afraid.

I bend
and kiss my mother's cheek.
"I will always love you, Mom."

I reach over
and shut
off
the machine.

When I open the door
to leave,
I notice,
I finally fit
into the shoes
my mother gave me.